The Tale of Fearsome Fritz

A Beaver Book

Published by Arrow Books Limited,
62-5 Chandos Place, London WC2N 4NW
An imprint of Century Hutchinson Ltd
London Melbourne Sydney Auckland
Johannesburg and agencies throughout the world

First published by Andersen Press 1982
Sparrow edition 1984
Beaver edition 1986

Text © Jean Willis 1982
Illustrations © Margaret Chambelain 1982

Printed in Italy by Grafiche AZ, Verona

ISBN 0 09 936300 3

The Tale of Fearsome Fritz

Words by
Jeanne Willis

Pictures by
Margaret Chamberlain

Beaver Books

This is the tale of Fearsome Fritz
Who scared his folks out of their wits.

He'd hide in cupboards, then jump out
In a dreadful mask, with a curdling shout.

Or he'd squirt himself with a red ink pot
And roll on the floor and pretend to be shot.

But the silliest thing he was ever to do
Was wear a gorilla suit into the zoo.

Of course, his mum would not have guessed,
He left the house quite neatly dressed.

Some rails at the back of the zoo were wide,
So Fritz, unnoticed, squeezed inside,

Slipped on the suit and hid, prepared
To make his victims good and scared.

A lady passed with a large ice cream.

Oh dear, you should have heard her scream!

When Fritz leapt on her, all she'd shout
Was, "A GORILLA HAS GOT OUT!"

The keeper thought she must be dreaming,
Drunk or mad with all that screaming.

Went to see, but in his rage
Forgot to lock the gorilla cage.

Now, while a crowd had gathered round
The fainting woman on the ground,

A real gorilla did escape
And off he went, this hairy ape

With massive leaps and bounds and swings
To where young Fritz had changed his things.

When the keeper found the cage was bare
And no gorilla was in there,
He told the lady she'd been right,
And, "Sorry for the nasty fright."

And with the help of several men
He vowed to catch the beast again.

Well, everyone was thrilled to bits,
Except, of course, for silly Fritz

Who wound up under lock and key
Where the gorilla used to be.

Meanwhile, Fritz's mum was cross.
Where Fritz was, she was at a loss.

"I'll go to the zoo. He must be told,"
She said, "his tea is getting cold."

"Oh, there he is, the naughty chap!"
She said, "I recognise that cap."
She smacked his legs and with a hiss,
Said, "Wait till Father hears of this."

"He's bound to have one of his fits."
Indeed he did. It wasn't Fritz.

Other titles in the
Beaver/Sparrow Picture Book series:

Use Your Head, Dear   Aliki
The Bad Babies Counting Book   Tony Bradman and Debbie van der Beek
Crazy Charlie   Ruth Brown
The Grizzly Revenge   Ruth Brown
If At First You Do Not See   Ruth Brown
The Big Sneeze   Ruth Brown
What's Inside   Satoshi Kitamura
In the Attic   Hiawyn Oram and Satoshi Kitamura
Ned and the Joybaloo   Hiawyn Oram and Satoshi Kitamura
The Adventures of King Rollo   David McKee
The Further Adventures of King Rollo   David McKee
The Hill and the Rock   David McKee
I Hate My Teddy Bear   David McKee
King Rollo's Play Room   David McKee
King Rollo's Letter   David McKee
Not Now Bernard   David McKee
Tusk Tusk   David McKee
Two Monsters   David McKee
The Truffle Hunter   Inga Moore
The Vegetable Thieves   Inga Moore
Babylon   Jill Paton Walsh and Jennifer Northway
The Tiger Who Lost His Stripes   Anthony Paul and Michael Foreman
The Hunter and the Animals   Tomie de Paola
The Magic Pasta Pot   Tomie de Paola
Mary Had a Little Lamb   Tomie de Paola
The Boy Who Cried Wolf   Tony Ross
Goldilocks and the Three Bears   Tony Ross
The Three Pigs   Tony Ross
Terrible Tuesday   Tony Ross and Hazel Townson
Emergency Mouse   Bernard Stone and Ralph Steadman
Inspector Mouse   Bernard Stone and Ralph Steadman
Quasimodo Mouse   Bernard Stone and Ralph Steadman
Mucky Mabel   Jean Willis and Margaret Chamberlain